Shop with Minnie

Adapted by Andrea Posner-Sanchez
Illustrated by Loter, Inc.

 A GOLDEN BOOK • NEW YORK

randomhouse.com/kids
ISBN: 978-0-7364-3031-9
Printed in the United States of America
10

Minnie has invited her friends to see the new items in her store.

"I have bows and bow ties of all shapes, colors, and sizes," Minnie says. "Please come in and shop."

Mickey, Donald, Daisy, Goofy, Pluto, Clarabelle, and Pete all head into Minnie's Bow-tique.

Everyone starts to look around.
"Gawrsh, Minnie!" says Goofy. "I love
your butterfly bows."

Minnie hands Goofy a butterfly net. "I'm
having a special today," she tells him. "You
can keep all the butterfly bows you catch."

Pete wants to find a birthday present for his aunt. There are so many bows to choose from! He leans over a display to reach for a pretty striped bow and . . .

. . . accidentally knocks all the bows down!
Pete feels bad about making a mess.

Luckily, everything is soon back where it belongs. Pete doesn't want to make any more messes. He decides to see which bows everyone else plans to get. Maybe that will help him find one for his aunt.

Minnie is a great salesperson.
She helps everyone find the bows
that are just right for them.
    Pluto has a bone bow—perfect
for a fancy pup!

Donald's bow tie doesn't just look great—it also takes pictures. It's a camera bow!

"Say 'cheese,'" Donald calls out to his friends.

"Attention, everyone!" Mickey loves that his bow tie makes his voice loud enough for everyone to hear. It's a microphone bow!

Clarabelle is crazy about her one-of-a-kind bow. When she sprays it with water, it grows flowers. It's a grow bow!

"Oh, Goofy!" Mickey announces with his microphone bow. "There are more butterfly bows for you to catch."

"This is more fun than a circus!" Goofy
exclaims as two butterfly bows flutter on his
arms. "Look, everyone—el*bows*!"

"My new bow makes me very happy," Daisy says to Minnie. "I can tell," Minnie replies. "It's a mood bow."

When Daisy is happy,
the mood bow is yellow.

When Daisy is sad,
the bow will turn blue.

When she is angry,
the bow will turn red.

Minnie models her store's fanciest bow.
It's a sparkling, shining disco bow!

All the bows in Minnie's Bow-tique are great, but Pete still doesn't know which one to get for his aunt. Then he spots a colorful bow with a switch attached to it. Pete gives the switch a tug and the bow starts spinning. It's a fan bow!

The fan spins faster and faster. It's making everything blow away! Finally, Pete is able to turn the bow off.

Everyone rushes to gather up the bows and return them to the store.

Minnie apologizes to her friends. "I'm sorry about the fan bow," she tells them. "I haven't figured out how to get it to work properly yet."

"I think it's perfect!" cries Pete. "My aunt will love it just the way it is."

He shows Minnie a picture of his aunt.

"She works in a hot kitchen all day long. A fan bow will be the best birthday present ever!"

Minnie is thrilled that all her friends found bows they like at her bow-tique.